It Takes Two

It Takes Two

by
JULIA BAZNIK

Foreword by
PAT A. HARGIS

RESOURCE *Publications* • Eugene, Oregon

IT TAKES TWO

Copyright © 2021 Julia Baznik. All rights reserved. Except for brief quotations in critical publications or reviews, no part of this book may be reproduced in any manner without prior written permission from the publisher. Write: Permissions, Wipf and Stock Publishers, 199 W. 8th Ave., Suite 3, Eugene, OR 97401.

Resource Publications
An Imprint of Wipf and Stock Publishers
199 W. 8th Ave., Suite 3
Eugene, OR 97401

www.wipfandstock.com

PAPERBACK ISBN: 978-1-7252-9594-0
HARDCOVER ISBN: 978-1-7252-9593-3
EBOOK ISBN: 978-1-7252-9595-7

04/14/21

Scripture quotations are from The ESV® Bible (The Holy Bible, English Standard Version®), copyright © 2001 by Crossway, a publishing ministry of Good News Publishers. Used by permission. All rights reserved.

Scripture quotations from The Authorized (King James) Version. Rights in the Authorized Version in the United Kingdom are vested in the Crown. Reproduced by permission of the Crown's patentee, Cambridge University Press. Used by permission. All rights reserved.

I dedicate this book first and foremost to my Lord and Savior, Jesus Christ. I also dedicate this book to the sweetest family and friends that a person could ask for. Life is blessed because all of you are in it. I love you all!

If we say we have no sin, we deceive ourselves, and the truth is not in us. (1 John 1:8 ESV)

The heart is deceitful, above all things, and desperately sick; who can understand it. (Jeremiah 17:9 ESV)

None is righteous, no, not one. (Romans 3:10 ESV)

For the wages of sin is death, but the free gift of God is eternal life in Christ Jesus our Lord. (Romans 6:23 ESV)

Contents

Foreword by Pat A. Hargis | ix
Preface | xiii
Acknowledgments | xv
Abbreviations | xvi
Introduction | xvii

CHAPTER ONE: Judah's Story | 1
CHAPTER ONE: Benji's Story | 3
CHAPTER TWO: Judah Again | 5
CHAPTER TWO: Benji Again | 7
CHAPTER THREE: Judah Says | 9
CHAPTER THREE: Benji Says | 11
CHAPTER FOUR: Judah's Back | 13
CHAPTER FOUR: Benji's Back | 15
CHAPTER FIVE: Judah's Thoughts | 17
CHAPTER FIVE: Benji's Thoughts | 19
CHAPTER SIX: Judah's Fear's | 21
CHAPTER SIX: Benji's Joys | 23
CHAPTER SEVEN: Judah's Pain | 25
CHAPTER SEVEN: Benji's Confliction | 28
CHAPTER EIGHT: Judah's Peace | 30
CHAPTER EIGHT: Benji's Peace | 32
CHAPTER NINE: Judah Gives In | 33

CHAPTER NINE: Benji Gives In | 35
CHAPTER TEN: Judah Must Go | 36
CHAPTER TEN: Benji Doesn't Know | 38
CHAPTER ELEVEN: Judah's Torment | 39
CHAPTER TWELVE: Judah Sees | 41
CHAPTER TWELVE: Benji Sees | 43
CHAPTER THIRTEEN: Judah Is Confused | 45
CHAPTER THIRTEEN: Benji Is Confused | 48
CHAPTER FOURTEEN: Judah Can't Find the Answer | 50
CHAPTER FOURTEEN: Benji Finds the Answer | 52
CHAPTER FIFTEEN: Benji and Judah | 55
CHAPTER SIXTEEN: Just Judah | 61

Foreword

PAT A. HARGIS
Emeritus Professor of English, Judson University

I was delighted to receive an email from Julia Baznik, a former student, in February of 2021 indicating that she would soon be publishing one of her fiction pieces, and I was honored to have her ask if I might provide a brief foreword. I wondered why, of course, since publishers prefer to include forewords by well-known names that will help get readers' attention. And I am quite sure that mine will not.

Apparently as one of her professors I had made more of an impression than I remembered—and let me note that while she graduated only five years ago, scores of intervening students tend to push out recollections of earlier ones. My immediate memories brought up the picture of a bright and hard-working student who had written a really good senior research project on language learning, though I did not recall feeling especially important in her development. So I thought it best to look through my records for a little more information.

While there were four full-time professors in Judson's English department at the time, as well as a variety of adjuncts, Julia's particular interests actually landed her in seven of my classes during her sophomore, junior, and senior years (rather than the three or four that most English majors would have needed and tolerated). And, given the vagaries of requirements and course scheduling, the poor girl had three of them in the same semester during her junior year. It appears that part of my influence was sheer quantity.

Perhaps the content of the courses had something to do with the impression. Two were rooted in linguistics. "Language and Society" and "The Nature of Language" encouraged deep reflection on our literary medium, as well as exploring its connection to the *imago Dei*. One was my favorite writing class, "Advanced Essay Writing," which explored and practiced the personal essay from its inception well into the 20th century. I hope the principle of "organic form" and the cadences of writers like Virginia Woolf, E. B. White, and Annie Dillard also got into Julia's psyche. Two more were classes developed out of my background in theology and literature, "Faith and Doubt" and "The Inklings." Perhaps reading a substantial number of Christian classics and spending a semester with C. S. Lewis, J. R. R. Tolkien, and Charles Williams whetted her appetite to do more fiction writing. And I can't help but wonder if there are some intentional echoes of Lewis and Williams in *It Takes Two*. If I helped make such connections, so much the better.

Whatever may have prompted her invitation, she has sparked my memoir impulse, and I offer a few more recollections of her—though note that my interaction with her was exclusively in and around the classroom. The picture should be filled out with the observations of what she was like at home, in the dorm, at the dining hall, in the chapel, in small groups, at work, in the community, etc., as well as what she is like today, of course.

My reading of her personality suggested that she was shy and introverted—perhaps even a little reclusive. No doubt she was also outgoing and expansive at times, but I think this Julia only showed up in small circles of close friends and family. She also struck me as sensitive and vulnerable—closely attuned to the concerns and pain of others. I also suspect that there was a Puckish, mischievous spirit—a manifestation of our "better angels," in my mind—behind her eyes, which likely only came out in ways that no one else would know about.

I can only hope that *It Takes Two* comes from the fiction writer's ability to observe and imagine, rather than paying the obligatory epic visit to the underworld. But even if that is the case, I also remember a sense that, beyond human happiness and unhappiness, Julia knew the unshakeable faith and joy that come from resting in the hands of God. And I am very pleased to see her writing in this vein.

Preface

Sometimes stories come to you in a second, whereas others seem to grow over a span of months, or even years. My story was envisioned in my mind for many months and then all at once was written down. A lot of times, it is not known why a story is written. Maybe, an author has had some of the same experiences that the main characters have, or they know of someone else's story that is similar to the character's story. Even though the meaning behind the story is not always known, the emotions and feelings are usually felt by the author. I wrote this book with the understanding of knowing what it feels like to be lost. To not know who you really are and what your life actually means. We are only on this earth for a short time; and in that short time we experience so much heartache and difficulty. Sometimes that is all we can see. Without Jesus Christ, life might simply consist of achievements and goals but those end up falling short as well. I wrote this book with the goal in mind of showing that nothing can truly be healed. Nothing can truly be revealed or made right without the great sacrifice of Jesus Christ, the Son of God.

Acknowledgments

First, I would like to thank my mom and dad for supporting me throughout this difficult writing process. Thank you for reading my book and giving me some much-needed constructive criticism.

I want to thank my boyfriend, Riley, for reading my book, as well, and giving me a lot of helpful insight. I really appreciate it. It made me think a little bit more outside of my box. Thank you for helping me to have a more positive outlook on life!

Thank you to all my coworkers for all your encouragement. It means a lot to me!

Thank you, Wipf and Stock Publishers, for giving me a chance. I really appreciate it!

Thank you, Wipf and Stock Publishers' editorial team for all of your help. I definitely needed it!

Thank you, Matt, Wipf and Stock's editorial production manager, for all your help and for answering all my questions. It means a lot.

I want to thank my professors and mentors at Judson University for all your help and insight over the four years that I was there. You gave me the strength to continue with this writing process until I finally succeeded.

And thank you, Lord Jesus, for your many blessings! You will always be my inspiration, my Savior, and my purpose in life. Without you, I am nothing.

Abbreviations

ESV   English Standard Version
KJV   King James Version

Introduction

Judah

Most people see children as innocent. Maybe not the kindest or gentlest creatures, but some sort of purity or innocence is in them. Until, they grow up. However, if you are surrounded by evil, since the moment you were born, that innocence and bright-eyed curiosity are exchanged with pure evil. And that is how my story starts. I came into this world with no name. I was left in a place crawling with insects and the smell of human feces. I am not sure how long I was there until I was found. But I do know that I was almost dead. My first year of life was spent in a foster care facility, until I was adopted by a single woman, in her late twenties.

This woman seemed to care about me for the first couple of years that I was with her. But she became more and more lax as the years went by. She would spend many a night going to parties at friends' houses, either leaving me at home or taking me with her. She and her friends would drink and sometimes do drugs. When I got a bit older, like seven or eight, her friends would offer me sips of their drinks, causing me to eventually start a ruckus, after too many sips. This ended up with me being placed in one of the friend's bedrooms until it was time to go home.

My mom, throughout my growing up years, didn't seem to care what I did or how I acted; as long as it didn't get in the way of her social activities. I never hated her. I just knew I never wanted to be like her. Unfortunately, since she was my one and only role model, since I was otherwise alone most of the time, besides her,

Introduction

I never had a chance to be the person I wanted to be. I never had that childlike wonder and innocence. All there was, was an acceptance of what I was to become. A selfish monster. Just like my so-called mom.

Benji

I remember being curious from a young age. Everything around me filled me with wonder. I remember sitting in my stroller, at our local park, trying to reach out and touch the pink flowers that were sprouting nearby. My mom saw my little fingers trying to graze those precious flowers, so she plucked them up for me, holding them up to my nose, so I could smell that delicious scent. My mom and dad allowed me to be curious, but they made sure I was respectful too.

To be gentle when I touched the flowers. To be kind when I asked my friends questions. But to keep that naive, childlike wonder on into adulthood. Through my parents' patience, love, and example, I was able to stay innocent. To not keep my heart corrupted, as I grew from a boy into a man. I know I am fortunate that I was adopted into the family that I was. That I grew up in a quiet countryside, surrounded by dirt roads and cornfields. Where I had room to ride my bike, to swim in the nearby pond, to live a quiet, simple life. My parents gave me that, and for that, I'm truly grateful. Who knows what would have happened to me if my parents hadn't chosen me.

CHAPTER ONE

Judah's Story

I like to sit inside an abandoned church in our neighborhood. Most of the stained glass windows are shattered, but there is one that is still intact. I like to sit on the broken pew next to the stained glass and look at the colors reflecting on me and around me and drink. There are a dozen of us who like to lounge around, in that old church, and drink and get high. Some shuffle around in a foggy haze. Others are almost scholarly, seeming to know all the solutions to the heavy burdens that life brings. Most of us really don't have anything going for us, no job, no future. No money to go to a community college, or trade school. High school is done and gone, and we have no idea what to do next. We end up drinking, doing drugs, and some of us even play instruments. So sometimes we have jam sessions. When we need something, we usually get it from home or take it from some store nearby. All of us don't really want to go home, mostly because nobody will be there anyway. Or the people who are at home are people we don't want to see. So we just hang out—day and night—pretending that we have some sort of meaning in our sad, pathetic lives.

I'm not saying that our hideout is all that great. It's filled with a bunch of selfish, miserable people, so there are always bound to be countless fights and arguments. Shoplifting is tricky, too, because it is hard not to get caught, especially with all the video cameras in every store and gas station in the area. The ones who are better at stealing have more food and belongings, causing contention when it comes to others coveting and trying to steal those belongings. All in all, staying here or going home, both options aren't great.

CHAPTER ONE

Benji's Story

The start of summer consisted of hours and hours of riding my bike around the dirt paths of our small town. Sometimes my friends would join me. We would bike around until we got worn out. Finally, crashing under a tree to eat the food that we had packed. We ate with gusto, sharing our dreams and plans for the future. School was about to end and we had so much planned and desired for our future. Some of my friends had ridiculous dreams, like becoming actors, or full-time webtoonists, but we decided to cheer them on because you never know what is possible in this life.

As for me, my parents and I sat down at our kitchen table, late one night, and planned a course of action for my future. My dream is probably just as ridiculous as becoming an actor or a webtoonist, but no matter how many times a day I tried to find another dream, goal, or passion, I just couldn't. This is what I want. This is what I desire and long for. I am going to become a journalist. Travel the world, and bring to light the beauty and the depth of this complicated world. But for now, the first plan of action is to go to community college and get all the general credits out of the way. And then from there, university. From there internships. And then from there, who knows. I just know it's going to be incredible.

As I lay down in the grass, listening to my friends laughing and chatting, filled with so much excitement, I couldn't help but feel an overwhelming mixture of anxiety and a complete thrill of what would happen next. I had so much going for me. I couldn't waste this precious time. But I was going to enjoy every second, as well. Like the clouds drifting above my head, so were the seconds of my life drifting by. I had to embrace every cloud, every second, before they drifted by. I couldn't wait for what was going to happen next.

CHAPTER TWO

Judah Again

Food was getting scarce and the rats were not helping. The church had seen better days, with its leaky roof and the rats rushing from pew to pew. The cross that was hanging in the pulpit area, or whatever you call it, was starting to fall apart. Everything was in disarray, and because of the heavy rain, we were all stuck inside, meaning more fights breaking out, and more food getting stolen. I finally decided I had enough of this. I would get more food before everyone started killing each other.

So, out into the pouring rain, I went. My hoodie doing very little to protect me. When I ended up at a nearby gas station, my shoes, pants, underwear, everything, were soaked. I was really regretting this decision, but we needed food. There was only one person besides me at the gas station. And the cashier was busy talking on her phone. Perfect. I scoured the store for cameras, spotting only two. Even better. I had a plastic bag with me, looking like I was just shopping around and would eventually pay for everything.

I had to keep my eyes on the cashier, customer, and cameras, without looking suspicious. Canned goods—check. Chips—check. Anything I could stuff into my bag—check. The other customer had left, and the cashier had turned, momentarily, still talking on her phone. This was it. I pulled my hood down, so the cameras wouldn't catch my face. Then I booked it. As fast as I could out the doors, into the pouring rain. The cashier turned to catch me exiting the gas station's doors, not realizing what was happening until I was already a distance away. I could hear her yelling after me, not even bothering to chase me. I was in the clear. But I continued to run. Making sure to look behind me to see if police or anyone else was following. But now what was important was that we were going to be okay. We would survive another week or two. Until, this awful weather died down. That's all that mattered.

CHAPTER TWO

Benji Again

I had finally started my classes at community college. I am kind of shy when it comes to meeting new people; so, the first couple of classes were kind of awkward. Hovering in the back of the classroom, trying to figure out who to sit by and who would not want me to sit next to them. I'd eventually always end up sitting in the last row, nearest to the door, just in case I needed to make a smooth and swift exit. But I guess a lot of my classmates had the same idea as me.

Every class period, I had the same people sit next to me, making my row full. And those people all seemed to know each other, and for some weird, unknown reason, they wanted to be friends with me too. The person who sat next to me first was April. She just plopped herself down, right next to me and smiled. "Hi, my name's April. What's your name?" From there, she introduced her three friends and her brother. "This is Crystal, Tammy, Joe, and my twin brother, Adam. Now you've met everyone. And everyone, this is Benji." I had never met a group of people who sat in the back row who were so outgoing and kind.

They instantly wanted me to hang out with them, form study sessions with them, and go out to eat with them. I didn't know why April wanted to be my friend. I didn't even look at her when she had sat down next to me. I even scooted my chair over a little bit. I don't get it. But I am thankful. We helped each other prepare for tests and quizzes. I even had another class with April, "Introduction to Geography."

April was also going to community college before she went to university. She still didn't know what school she wanted to go to. She said she wanted to go to a university that really helped in the financial aid department. As I started to get to know her, I think I was starting to like her more and more. Whatever university she decides to go to I think I want to go to the same one. Obviously, her brother and her want to go to the same school. And Adam is a really nice guy too, so of course, that would be a plus. Learning about Calculus, History, Psychology, Speech 101, and English, has actually been a lot better than I thought it would be, now that I met April. I think this is going to be a really good year.

CHAPTER THREE

Judah Says

The day finally happened. We were ratted out, about our hideout. A lot of us staying in the church are underage, so that meant police had to get involved, either tracking down the kids' parents or worse, sending them into foster care. None of us wanted this to happen. Yes, we fought a lot, but we still cared for each other, much more than our own families ever would. But before we knew it, we were torn apart, separated. I felt completely responsible.

As one of the oldest ones there, I should have been more on my guard, especially with the stealing. I should have warned the younger ones to not get too rowdy and loud when they drank. When they fought too, I should have broken up the fights more quickly. But I couldn't. I could barely hold myself together. I hated who I was and what I had become.

I was so angry about my lot in life, I didn't care about anyone or anything. I just wanted an escape from it all. I wanted to stop thinking about myself and my problems, but that's all that raced through my head, day in and day out. But honestly, I have so little going for me, there isn't much else to think about. It's mostly about the injustice of it all.

Why did I have to be adopted in a home where my mom cared nothing for me? She probably didn't even realize that I had left. Why did my birth mother abandon me in a state of filth and squalor, leaving me to die that way? Why was my only role model such a selfish person? It makes me so sick that I'm becoming more and more like her everyday! It's just not fair! I didn't even have a chance to be a good person from the moment I was born, up until now! It's just not fair! I want another life!

CHAPTER THREE

Benji Says

Finals are nearing, and I have decided to go to DePaul University with April and Adam. Crystal, Tammy, and Joe are going to be going to a smaller college in southwest Indiana. It's a long trip, but we all decided to meet up during the summer break. Both April and I got accepted into DePaul, but Adam is on the waiting list. This has been tough for April because she has never been away from her brother before. This has mostly been all she can talk about when we talk on the phone. I understand. I may not have siblings, but I'm going to miss my parents so much when I go off to university in the fall.

It's not like I can't talk to them on the phone but not being able to talk to them face-to-face is really hard to think about. I don't know how I'll handle that. Not being able to go fishing with my dad every weekend. Just talking about life, meaning, purpose, stuff like that with him. Not being able to go on nature walks with my mom. We both like birds so much.

When I was little, my mom got a book from the library that played off different bird calls, so you could recognize birds by their calls, more easily. We spent several weeks, almost every day, trying to figure out what birds we heard. I'll miss that beautiful stillness and solitude most of all. Chicago, I've heard, is loud, and chaotic. I'm definitely scared, but I know this is the school that April and

Adam want to go to, so I'm going to go as well. I'm going to stay optimistic, no matter what! It will be fun ... Hopefully.

CHAPTER FOUR

Judah's Back

Back again, to that unforgiving house. Too old for foster care, too dead inside for any type of fast food job. I have no credit, no money. Low-income housing won't accept me, because of my past records, including theft and assault charges. I had no choice but to come back. Either here or a homeless shelter. If it gets really bad, I'll go to a shelter. But for now, I'm stuck here. So there I was, sitting in that living room, furniture looking as old and battered as ever. My mom was sitting in that old, brownish-gray armchair, beer in her hand, surrounded by her creepy friends. It was like I had never left. They still offered me drinks, trying to get me drunk, to see me do something stupid. They still talked a lot but were really saying absolutely nothing. My mom, like always, acted like I wasn't there unless she wanted me to get something for her. Her friends just saw me as the same stupid, little kid, who was there to entertain them.

    As I started to drift in and out of sleep, they kicked me to see if they could get a reaction out of me. I eventually forced myself to get up and go to sleep, with the drunken protests of her friends, calling me names. They just wanted me to come back and be their little show-monkey. That night, in my drunken state, I thought up ways that I could get rid of my mom and her friends. In all my years, I had never thought of killing anyone, but that night, for hours, I plotted on how to kill her. In a way that wouldn't look like murder. If this all worked out, I would then inherit her house and her money. This was only fair, after how she has treated me, like nothing, like filthy garbage, all these years. It would take a while to plan out, but eventually, everything would fall into place. Everyone would get what they deserve. Whether that would be a house, money, or death.

CHAPTER FOUR

Benji's Back

Adam was not accepted into DePaul University. April was devastated but decided to still go, after a lot of convincing from Adam and her parents. Over the summer months, I continued to grow closer to April, as well as Adam. As I grew closer to them, I started to do what they did and liked what they liked. Both of them are pretty religious. Their family goes to church regularly. Also, Bible studies on Wednesday and Saturday. Their family even reads the Bible together and watches Christian movies. I've never been to church before, nor have I really been interested in it much. My parents always told me that being a good person is enough; so I've always just tried to be respectful of all living things.

Now, after going to church, I'm told, I'm not a good person, even though I've always been kind and respectful. In fact, I'm a sinner. A wicked person who deserves hell. And God's Son, Jesus, died for me, so I wouldn't have to go to hell. If I believe that Jesus is God's Son and that he died for my sins, I can go to heaven. I also have to confess my sins and repent. Then I am saved from eternal death in hell. Yeah.

When I heard all of this, I was dumbstruck. My parents aren't bad people. I'm not a bad person. I've never intentionally done anything bad. April is a good person and so is Adam. I just didn't get it. But I told April, the day after they took me to church, that I believed in what their pastor had said, that I was a sinner and that

I believed that Jesus died for my sins and rose from the dead after three days. That I was sorry for my sins and wanted Jesus to save me and be in my life.

    I don't know why I said that. I think I was afraid of losing April and Adam. Especially, April, because I am kind of falling in love with her. I couldn't tell them that their religion made no sense to me, and seemed to be made up of a bunch of ridiculous stories. I cared so much about them and what they think of me, so I lied. I am so afraid of losing them, that I lied. So I guess I became a fake Christian. I guess that does kind of make me a bad person.

CHAPTER FIVE

Judah's Thoughts

The thought of murder didn't leave my mind. When I was lying down and when I was waking up, that was all I could think about. And as I thought of clever ways to murder my mom, my bitterness and resentment for her continued to grow. It became like a type of leech or bug in my ear, whispering to me, reminding me of all the times she had neglected and abandoned me. Treated me like a flea-infested dog. Or like a flea, itself.

This nagging, bug-like voice was constantly in my ear, no matter how much I ignored it. No matter how much I tried to get it to go away. It wouldn't. I began to feel like I really would kill my mom if this didn't let up. So, I decided to stay away from her as much as possible.

I usually ended up wandering around our neighborhood, going from street to street. Weaving through alleyways, sitting in parks, trying to think about anything else, except for what was going on in my head.

I watched kids running around the park, drifting from the swings to the slide to the monkey bars and back again. Parents were smiling and laughing with each other, and the babies who were too young were napping in their strollers. I can't remember a time when my mom had brought me to a park. Well, she did once, but she got bored and we had to leave after about five minutes.

Whenever I asked her to take me to a park again, she would always say it was a waste of her time. She's too busy. Busy doing what?

Once I even ran away to go to a park, myself, since she wouldn't take me. That was the best day of my life. All the neighborhood kids were so much fun to play with. I wanted a lot of attention, so I was really loud, energetic, and talkative, and all of my new friends thought I was hilarious. I was even outgoing with the parents, showing them all of my sad, pathetic cartwheels and handstands. They clapped for me and told me how sweet and handsome I was. I had never had that much loving attention before. It felt like I was eating some delicious candy, but even better than that. I wished every day was like that. Unfortunately, they eventually found out that I had come to the park alone. And after a lot of convincing, they finally got my mom's number out of me. That day was too short.

As I sat in that park, trying to ignore those awful bugs whispering in my head, I wished for that day to come back.

CHAPTER FIVE

Benji's Thoughts

My whole body was submerged into water, as April's pastor dunked me into the icy cold river, in our town. I am just glad I agreed to get baptized in the middle of summer. As I came back up out of the water, I saw the smiling faces of the pastor, April, Adam, their parents, and the rest of the congregation. I felt a sick lump in my throat, almost as if I was going to gag or vomit. I know I had taken it too far, but to justify my actions, I did believe in Jesus and God, and I did believe in heaven. I just didn't believe that all people were wicked and deserving of hell. And I did not believe that good people needed to repent of their sins. I'm sure Jesus did die for certain people's sins, like murderers, rapists, and those sorts of awful people, who really do deserve hell. But people like me, April, Adam, my high school friends, my parents, if we have been living good moral lives, I'm sure God would understand. So, I do think I am a Christian.

I may not agree with everything the pastor has taught us, but most of it I do agree with, so technically, I'm not deceiving April and her family, right? But still, I feel sick, very sick.

April did explain, a couple weeks ago, that her father needed some type of external proof that I was a Christian before he gave us permission to date, so I had to do this. Right? I'm not sure. But April means so much to me. I can't lose her. And Adam has become a really good friend. I've even taken him fishing with my dad and me. Something I have never done before, not even with my high school buddies. Yeah, my dad and Adam did go back and forth with the religious stuff, but they decided to just respect each other's views.

I think Adam saw he was getting nowhere with my dad and just gave up. I haven't told my parents I became a "Christian." I'm not sure how they would react since they didn't have any religious views while I was growing up. I was just told to be a good person and to do what made me happy, as long as it did not hurt anyone around me. I think they will support me, as long as I do not impose my views on them.

After Adam left, my dad told me that he liked him, he just didn't like how Christians are so pushy with their religion. "Christians would be alright if they weren't so pushy and respected other people's views and opinions. I could actually be friends with Christians if they were more like that." I decided that I wasn't lying to April and Adam, I was just my own Christian. Maybe a bit less conservative than them, but essentially believing the same thing. But for some reason after the baptism, after dinner with April's family, after the long bike ride home, and after I lay down to sleep, something deep down inside of me still felt so sick. Like I knew deep down inside that something was very wrong. I just didn't know what it was.

CHAPTER SIX

Judah's Fear's

The park, my favorite place to go, wasn't even helping with my restless mind. Restlessly pacing up and down the sidewalks while talking to myself didn't help either. People began giving me fearful looks. Parents would even pulled their kids closer to themselves and away from me. In fear that I might snatch their kids or something. Some people even crossed to the opposite sidewalk when they saw me whispering and muttering to myself. But that's the only way I could think of to counteract the thirst for blood that was inside of me. To reason and rationalize loudly to myself. To verbalize that I was not a murderer, even though my mind wanted me to think I was.

So, I tried to go to secluded sidewalks and alleyways and just fight with myself. It didn't help anything that I was trying not to drink away my problems. Instead I was trying to face them head-on. But I'm weak. I can't only just yell and scream. I need something to ease the pain.

Usually, when I returned home, my mom and her friends were all passed out in the living room. I would usually take what was left from their daily parties and finish it off in my room. That's how I made it through the night. And that's how I made it through the days, just waiting for the nights to come.

My fear continued to grow inside of me. I never wanted to become worse than my mom. But what if I did become worse?

Became a murderer. What's the point of living, if I become what my thoughts tell me that I am? I've already thought of many ways of murdering her. Does that mean I will actually act it out too? I'm scared. I'm scared of who I am and who I will become. But most of all I'm scared that there is no good left in me at all. I'm just . . . so afraid.

CHAPTER SIX

Benji's Joys

I can't believe it! Only a month away from the move to DePaul. After my baptism, it seemed like everything had fallen into place. My parents were fine with me becoming a Christian. They said they would support me in whatever decision I made. That fear vanished. Then April's father, after a lot of kind of intense discussion, agreed that April and I could date. And what tops it all off is that Adam got into Loyola University, which isn't too far from the school April and I are going to.

Honestly, April's dad seemed so relieved that Adam was going to go to a school in Chicago too. Even though he doesn't show it in front of April, I can tell he still doesn't trust me. Not really at all. I know this is April's first relationship, and she is his only daughter, so it is hard. But he acts like I'm this bad person. It's not like I've really been in a lot of relationships. But I'm not going to talk to April's dad about that. But other than that, everything is falling into place.

It does seem like God is watching out for me. I've been learning a lot more about God, Jesus, and the Bible. I think my favorite Bible character, so far, is David. How he killed Goliath, the giant, so easily, even though he was so young. And how everyone cowered in fear, yet he was so brave. I want that. To be brave and mighty like that. To stand strong in what I believe, even though I am still unsure what exactly to believe.

For now, I just want to be a kind and respectful son, friend, and boyfriend. I really do believe God will work everything out in the end, if I just simply do my part to make the world a better place. That's all I think God is asking of me and wants from me. He really has blessed me with everything I could ever want and need. And for that, I am so joyful.

CHAPTER SEVEN

Judah's Pain

I have found a hideout, once again. It's an old Catholic church, where very few people seem to enter its doors. When I first went through its doors, I was being plagued with thousands of evil thoughts at once, filling my entire mind, my body. I was so weak I could barely move, and chest so heavy I could barely breathe. The agony was so much I had to beat my fist against my heart to help ease the pain, and to help the turmoil to end in the only way I knew how. I saw the church with my bleary vision. The stone steps leading up to a vast church. But that wasn't what drew me to the church. Rather, at the front of the church, there was a large stained glass window. The window was a piercing dark red, the color of blood. But what drew my attention, even more, was the gold cross in the center. The sun was just about to set, and the sunbeams glared onto the gold cross, causing the colors to explode in my eyes. The cross was surrounded by blood but the light outshone the blood, making it almost seem to vanish in my eyes. I had to go in.

So I climbed each step, as my mind seemed to scream out louder and louder, but I kept going. I walked into the large church, met with many gold pews, and a red carpet running down the aisle. As I walked down the aisle, I saw stained glass windows and murals depicting the life of Jesus. I didn't know much about the Bible or Jesus, just a few stories I was told by some people who were witnessing on the street, a while back. It seemed like a bunch of garbage to me. But staring at these pictures, I felt something deep inside of me.

When I got to what I think is the altar, pulpit, whatever, something made me stop in my tracks. There it was again, a large gold cross, surrounded by blood, but this time the cross wasn't empty. Jesus was on that cross. He had thorns digging into the flesh of his head and blood dripping down his face. I could see the pain and suffering on that face. What was even worse were the nails in his hands. And one large nail going through both of his feet. What was more humiliating was there was only one single garment of cloth to cover himself.

He was put on that cross to die and be humiliated. From what I could remember from what those Christian people had told me, Jesus came to earth to die for us. Why would he come to this earth if he knew he was going to be murdered and die in such a humiliating way? I even remember them saying that he was God's Son. He is the Son of God, yet he chose to die like this? From the looks of it, he was tortured.

If I was a god, I wouldn't have even looked twice at this earth. I would have destroyed it. Been rid and done with all this mess. Who cares about these awful, awful people down on earth! I noticed a banner above the cross. In bright gold lettering it read, "For God So Loved The World He Gave His Only Begotten Son, That Whosoever Believeth In Him Shall Not Perish But Have Everlasting Life" (John 3:16 KJV). I have no idea what begotten meant, but one thing stuck with me. God so loved the world. God so loved the world that he gave Jesus and Jesus agreed to go and die? For the world? For Me? Why?

The thoughts began to swarm back into my head as I stared at the dying Jesus. I slumped into the pew, staring, though my vision was starting to get blurry again. As my head felt like it was about to explode, I looked at his blood-soaked face. "Jesus." I breathed out. In a second it seemed like the cross behind Jesus had started to glow, but I know I've already been starting to lose my mind, so it was probably a hallucination. But once I breathed out that name, something seemed to lift inside my mind.

    The terrible, murderous thoughts began to drift away. The soul-crushing pain inside my head began to drift away, as well. It was still. The room was still, my mind was still. Lights from the stained glass flickered onto my face as I looked back up to the cross. As I looked into the face of Jesus, I could almost see a faint smile, that hadn't been there before. I knew it was just a statue but it seemed like some sort of message. As if Jesus had really heard me. I felt myself unfold, crumble, and fall apart all at once. The tears I never let fall finally fell, as I looked into the smiling face of Jesus.

CHAPTER SEVEN

Benji's Confliction

As I grew closer and closer to April, I felt more and more guilty, especially since I was pretending to agree with everything that she believed in. We are only a month away from moving to Chicago, but this guilt is eating me up inside. If I tell her I'm not a Christian, in the way she wants me to be, I'll lose her for good.

I've been riding my bike, alone, across our dusty, dirt roads (it hasn't been raining lately). I ride past the cornfields, hidden pathways, and rivers, trying to figure out what to do. I am a good person, so something like this rips me up inside. I don't usually lie or leave out information, but I am in love with April and she is in love with me. Adam is one of my closet friends now, and even Adam and April's mom really likes me. I know everyone wants April and me to work out. Even my parents love April. My mom calls her sweetheart. That shows how much of a great person she is.

I've told April everything about myself. About my adoption and where I came from. Even though it's obvious that I've been adopted. I look nothing like my parents. April doesn't even push Christianity on my parents. She just talks about it with my parents, in a kind and subtle way. Everything about her is kind. I can't lose her just because of some differences in views and opinions. So, I'm just going to continue riding around on my bike, until this guilt disappears. Because, I'm never losing April. She's told me everything about herself, as well, and I've shared everything, except this.

We are connected in that way. It's got to mean something. It's got to mean something, especially since I may not really be a Christian. At least our hearts are connected, even though our souls may not be.

CHAPTER EIGHT

Judah's Peace

I sat in that church daily; just sitting. Looking at Jesus. His Father loved him. He cared about Jesus, yet God's love was so great that he sent Jesus to the world.

    I occasionally saw a caretaker come in and out of the church, while I was there. I finally worked up the nerve to ask him why God sent Jesus to the world to die. He explained to me about human sin. And how God is perfect and sin is against God, so, therefore, we are separated from God. God loved us so much that he sent Jesus to die for us so that we would no longer be separated from God and be able to go to heaven instead of going to hell.

    I've never had anyone love me before. People liked me, I guess, because I did things for them, like my mom, the kids that I lived with, in that old church, and my mom's stupid friends. They all only cared about me because I got more beers for them, or entertained them, or stole food for them. But I've never felt love, nor have I ever really loved anyone myself. But a God loved me? He turned his Son human and let him die because he loved me? That's something that makes no sense.

    I've heard stories about gods before, but they were always unfeeling and unloving. Tyrants who showed off their power and oppressed humans that were on earth. But a gentle and kind God? It's hard to believe, especially after everything I've been through. It seems like there is not a single cell of gentleness and kindness in this terrible world. But still every day, I came back. Because when I looked at Jesus hanging on that cross, I finally felt some peace.

CHAPTER EIGHT

Benji's Peace

I think more than having a religion, rules, or regulations, I think love is the best thing on earth. So, I'm at peace with everything. We are leaving in a couple of weeks! I can't wait!

CHAPTER NINE

Judah Gives In

I had gotten very drunk after my mom's friends had forced one too many drinks on me. They had drifted off into various rooms of the house, leaving me alone with my mom. I knew we shouldn't be alone together, especially because of how I had been feeling toward her for several months now. I hated her incessant talking about nothing, her complete lack of interest toward me, her constant asking for something; since she was too lazy to get it herself. I just hated her. But as I looked at her, I wondered how God could love her. It said God loved the whole world but people like this, they seemed so unlovable to me.

This woman had been chattering away for a while now, so I told her to shut up. She then proceeded to scream at me. Telling me that she should have never adopted me and that I never listen to her. Never do what she wants. She went on and on, yelling louder and louder. And my thoughts grew louder and louder, drowning out the name that I used every time I couldn't handle it anymore. In my drunken mind, I just knew I needed it to stop. Whatever it takes. Yes, she isn't ignoring me anymore, but this is far worse. So, without thinking I threw the nearest thing I could find at her. And that happened to be a beer bottle. I didn't look as I threw it. I just wanted quiet. And I did get quiet. I didn't look at her after I threw it. I just knew I needed somewhere to lie down to sleep it all off.

That night, my head was unusually quiet. And I finally slept well, for the first time in a long time.

CHAPTER NINE

Benji Gives In

I finally gave in and told April about my beliefs. That I believe most people are basically good inside and that those people don't have to repent for their sins. I was shaking, as I told her. I was going to lose this awesome girl, over something so stupid. April, however, didn't react in the way I thought she would.

"It's okay, Benji. I still love you." She said that with the sweetest smile. How lucky am I! She believed I was a Christian, just more liberal than her and her family. I just couldn't tell her parents or Adam about this. So I didn't.

I don't know what I was so afraid of. I should have told her before I was baptized about this. I told her I was sorry, over and over again, and over and over again, she said that she forgave me and that she loved me. And that's all I needed to hear.

Whenever her dad gives us permission, we bike down one of my favorite trails, before the sunsets, to my favorite maple tree near a lazy creek. While we bike, I can see the sun shining in her hair. She always bikes in front of me, making her blonde hair seem almost golden, in the sunlight. When we usually near my favorite tree, the sun has already set and the stars are just starting to stretch in the sky. We sit and talk underneath the tree. As I look into her eyes, I see the stars sparkling back at me and I know this is always where I want to be.

CHAPTER TEN

Judah Must Go

My mom hadn't moved out of her armchair. Shards of glass were in her hair. And there was dry blood that was caked onto her face and her neck. She didn't seem like she was breathing either. I put my fingers next to her nose to see if any air was coming out. There was nothing. I fell back onto the floor, my whole body shaking. I had been trying so hard not to give into my evil urges, yet in a moment of extreme weakness, I had unintentionally given in and killed her. I don't know what had come over me, since I had been so fascinated by God's love and the sacrifice of Jesus Christ, for our sins. But all of that seemed to leave my mind.

First, I was filled with intense fear. I was going to prison, especially because of all the other crimes I've committed. But something in me seemed to be resigned to what had happened. There was no hope for me from the start. I knew I was evil. It was just who I was. No matter how much I tried, I wouldn't be able to break away from this evil. Just like the writing on that church's banner said, without the sacrifice of Jesus, all people are going to perish and go to hell. I guess because of my crimes, I'm going to be heading into hell much faster than the average person. And I know for a fact, that my mom is already in hell.

But a part of me felt relief that I was done fighting. I knew I never would have won to begin with. I'm weak and selfish. That's all I am. God isn't going to forgive someone like me anyway. One good thing about this situation was that it didn't seem like murder. I couldn't have thought of a better scenario on my own. The whole murder scene seemed like it could have been some sort of drunken fight. Or she could have been so intoxicated that she did it to herself. Whatever the scenario, it was time to leave. I packed a few belongings, trying to decide where to go and what to do. When I left the house, I did not look back.

CHAPTER TEN

Benji Doesn't Know

It's still bothering me why April was so cool about my confession. The church, God, Jesus, all that stuff are the most important things in her life. She even told me that she loved me because I believed in all the truths that she does. But to see her act like its no big deal, seemed very odd to me. I know she loves me, but did she love me so much that she would compromise? I didn't think so. That's why I was expecting us to break up, or that I would have had to confess to her parents, or even that I would have to be counseled by her church's pastor. But she did none of that. She accepted it. Maybe she didn't really accept it but she's just too nice to tell me how she really feels. That sounds like April. She is super outgoing, but hates to hurt other people's feelings, or make anyone feel uncomfortable. I don't know what is going on inside her head. I hope she really has accepted what I believe. I hope this doesn't cause any tension or conflict between us, especially since we are leaving in a week. I just don't know.

CHAPTER ELEVEN

Judah's Torment

I ended up connecting with an old friend whose uncle lives in a little town in Illinois. He was already heading to his uncle's house, to help on his farm over the summer. My friend, James, told me his uncle wouldn't mind the extra help and I could sleep in the barn's loft. James didn't question why I needed somewhere to go and a job. He already knew what my mother was like and didn't ask for any type of explanation. I hadn't spoken to him for years, yet he still seemed to care for me. It's sad that we hadn't been in touch. He wasn't a bad guy. It's good I never deleted his number and that it had stayed the same, after all these years.

The car ride was quiet. James simply played some soft music as we drove on the highways that led to our destination, the middle of nowhere. I sat in the back seat, replaying in my mind how I found my mom. I asked Jesus for forgiveness, but I don't think he'll listen after what I have done. So I sat in torment, filled with guilt, trying not to listen to the bugs, that were now gnawing on my brain, trying to torment me once again. I kept saying the name "Jesus" in my head but it didn't seem to be helping this time around.

The drive was long and bumpy, filled with a lot of dirt roads, but we finally made it. As we went down a dirt path, I saw someone biking in the opposite direction pass us by. Time seemed to slow down as he passed the car. I could almost feel my heart stop beating in my chest. He was me. Same dark hair, same eyes, same skin, same everything. The only thing that was different was that he was wearing nicer clothes than me, and his hair was freshly cut. How could someone I didn't even know look exactly like me? Even his kind of bored-looking facial expression looked like mine.

"Hey." I looked more intently as he waved at someone. He even sounded kind of like me. As he disappeared out of sight, I was still frozen in place. What was that? Had I finally lost my mind?

CHAPTER TWELVE

Judah Sees

I've seen my twin, doppelganger, ghost, whatever it is, four times now. And every time I get close to it, it somehow gets away. It never notices me, but I can always see it. Maybe this vision or hallucination is punishment for my sins.

Because of this vision, I've been putting all my energy into farming. I didn't tell James about my visions. I don't want him to tell his uncle. I might lose my only place to stay and my job. So, I've kept silent.

All that I do is work on the farm. And at night, James and I just sit up, drink, and watch the stars. We both don't have much to say, but I think both of us have a lot we don't want to say. Maybe he is running from something too. At night though, in my dreams, I still see my mom's dead body. The scene switches to a dirt road, where I see the boy who looks just like me. I chase after him, but I'm on foot and he's on a bike. I run for what seems like miles, until I reach the church I had been going to for months, with the stained glass cross at the front. I walk down the aisle, once again. The church is dark, except for the cross, that is illuminated at the front. I sit down at the first pew, where I always sit, looking up into Jesus's face.

This time, however, as I look into his eyes, I see tears falling down his face, causing the blood to run down as well. I come to the realization that I have saddened a Savior. The world's Savior.

He loves me. Yet, I don't care anything for him. I wake up nightly, in a cold sweat, wishing I didn't have to see those tears anymore. They were unbearable.

CHAPTER TWELVE

Benji Sees

A few more days to go. I can't wait! DePaul here I come! I was on my way to meet April. It finally had rained, but that meant muddy terrain, making it much more difficult to ride my bike. But that didn't matter so much, as long as I got to see April. We were going to have a barbecue with her and her family. Kind of a way of sending us all off to university and the big city. My parents couldn't make it because of prior commitments but we were going to have our own farewell party, anyway.

As I rode, rather slowly, down the pathway toward the Donovans' farm, I saw a figure in the distance who seemed vaguely familiar. I had never seen him before but somehow I knew him. He was wearing simple-looking clothing and a cap on his head. As I drew nearer, my heart seemed to slow down and my breathing began to speed up. He lifted his face toward the sun, revealing his face fully to me. He was me. The same eyes, same hair, same smile, same olive skin, same everything. Of course, I dress better than him and my hair is much more maintained but all and all we were the same.

I kept staring as I passed him but he didn't even seem to notice me. I was so focused on him, that I let my bike slide on some mud, causing me to crash face-first on my bike. The pain in my knee was jarring but I quickly turned around to see if he was still there. He was not. It was just an empty field and an empty road.

The entire barbecue I couldn't think about anything else but that boy with my face. In the back of my mind, I wondered if my birth mother had had twins. I didn't know anything about her and honestly didn't want to know. But what if it wasn't just me in that abandoned building? What if I had had someone else by my side? Somehow the whole idea of moving to Chicago in a couple of days didn't sound so great. I had to find him.

CHAPTER THIRTEEN

Judah Is Confused

My fear seemed to grow in me daily. I had run away from my sins but they had just followed me to the middle of nowhere. Now my guilt was causing me to hallucinate regularly. Every time that I was with James and I saw my other self, I would ask him if he saw anything. And every time he said he didn't see anything. No matter where we were. On a dirt road, near his uncle's barn, every time it was, "No, I don't see anything." I had tried to escape, but my demons were going to follow me to the ends of the earth. So I stopped mentioning my hallucinations, fantasy, craziness, whatever, to James and focused all my energy on the Donovans' farm.

I worked without breaks, sunup to sundown, bailing hay, shoveling up the animals' feces, digging up weeds in James's aunt's garden. Whatever was asked of me, I did. And I did it gladly. Any distraction was well received. Anything to get my mind off of what I was becoming. That's what scared me most of all. Because I might already be the person I had never wanted to be. I might have already become that evil person I had feared I would become. It might already be too late to stop the inevitable. There was also something else that didn't sit right with me. And that was what James had said to me recently.

James and I were together in the cow's area of the barn, shoveling up the massive amounts of manure. A great time to have a conversation, I might add. It seemed to come out of nowhere. "So what's her name?" James asked after he had finished struggling to put a giant chunk of manure into the wheelbarrow, nearby. "Who?" I asked, too busy making a pile of manure. "You know. That girl. The one I saw you with." At that, I had completely stopped my scooping to look directly at him.

    I had not even once interacted with a single girl in this town. Yes, I had seen girls, when I went to James's uncle's church. It was a requirement that we went to their church if we wanted to stay in their house and work on their farm. This was after they had caught us drinking late one night in their barn. I had not talked to a single girl. I had kept to myself and even listened to the entire sermon. I wasn't going to be kicked out now, especially since I had nowhere else to go. The sermon was about repentance. How we are sinful and need to confess our sins to no longer be separated from God. I don't think this pastor meant everyone can get back into God's good graces after repentance. Probably only the good people out there can truly be free from their wrongs, who aren't murderers, like me. God gave his only Son for me. And what do I do to show my gratefulness? I go ahead and kill my mom. I don't think God's going to forgive something like that after everything he did for me. If I was God, I would never even look at one of my creations if they spit on my face like that.

    Anyway, where was I? Oh yeah, girls. When James asked me about a girl I was with, I was wondering if I was wearing off on him. Maybe he had started hallucinating too. "I don't know what you're talking about." James let out a sigh, sticking his shovel into the manure, so he could turn around and look at me. "Come on! Don't play dumb! I've seen you with her several times!" I stared at him even more intensely. Was he seeing what I had been seeing? Was he also seeing the other me? Or had I gone completely crazy and couldn't remember who I had been with and what I had been doing? I tentatively asked him, "What does she look like?" James literally smacked his hand onto his forehead, which honestly is disgusting, considering all the manure we had been touching.

    "You can't fool me. I've seen you two several times. Even my uncle has seen you two. It is obviously that blonde girl from church.

The skinny one that's really short. Her family is really involved in the church. She's got a twin brother." He picked up his shovel again, turning away from me. He muttered something under his breath that I pretended not to hear.

As we continued piling up the manure, I felt an intense queasiness in my stomach. Yes, I had seen this girl before. Yes, we had sat close to her and her family. But I had never talked to her. I had barely even looked at her. Yet, James had said I had been with her on several occasions. Maybe it had been my double, doppelganger, I don't know. Or maybe my mind had finally given up. Maybe, just maybe I was finally gone. I don't know. All I know was that I was confused.

CHAPTER THIRTEEN

Benji Is Confused

After that day, all I could think about was finding answers. DePaul seemed to have completely slipped my mind. I needed to know if there was someone else like me. Was there someone who shared the same experiences as I did? Was there not one but two of us, in that run-down place? Someone who shared the same face as me? What had happened to him? Was he as fortunate as me? Did he experience love and happiness like I did? Was he able to be curious and imaginative? Free to be himself? I hadn't really seen or talked with April for the last day and a half. Instead, I went to my parents.

My mind was buzzing with a million questions. I made sure we all sat down together and then I unloaded on them. I needed to know exactly where I was found. If there was anyone else found with me. Did they know if my birth mother had any other children? Did the adoption agency ever tell them if I had a twin? I had never really brought up my past. I was never very interested in finding more information. That is until now.

It seemed to startle my parents at first because I had always been so disinterested before. But being the parents that they are, they were willing to do anything to help me find answers. My parents truly are good people. I told them about the boy I saw who looked like me, exactly like me, making my parents more motivated to help me find answers. But everything seemed to lead to a dead end. The adoption agency confirmed that I was found alone. That there were no records stating that I had a twin. And it was unknown whether my birth mother had any other children. They didn't even know her whereabouts. So it seemed like our search was completely in vain. I knew the only thing left to do is to find him, whoever he was. If I don't find him, I'll be stuck in a state of confusion. Forever.

CHAPTER FOURTEEN

Judah Can't Find the Answer

I've been going by James's uncle's church when no one else is around. I usually go late at night. It's a very small town, so nobody locks anything. The doors are always open. This church is definitely not as lavish as the Catholic church in my old neighborhood but there is something so peaceful in the simplicity of this church. There is also a large cross on the stage. It is also gold, just a lot more simple. Like before, I sit at the front pew and look at that large, golden cross. And I talk with Jesus. I'm not sure if he is listening but I still talk. I tell him about how I think I am losing my mind, and I don't think I can stop it. I also apologize over and over again for what I did to my mom.

I know I won't be forgiven because I feel even more guilty after I apologized. But I continue to apologize anyway. Hopefully, one day I will be forgiven. But for now, I just feel immense, crushing guilt. I even tell him about my life. How much I hated it and how unfair it was.

Maybe I shouldn't be saying all of this to God because, well, he's God! But I need to tell someone. It will eat me up inside if I don't. But even after all of this talking, or praying, if you could call it that, I don't see or hear anything. It's not like my experience in the other church. Where I saw Jesus's smile and felt my demons being flung out of my mind. Now there is nothing. But still, I talk because I don't know what else to do. I can't rely on myself because

I am a ticking time bomb. And I can't rely on anyone, not even James, because I'll lose everything if anyone knows who I am and what I have done. So I talk. I yell. I plead. I even cry, the thing I hate doing the most.

But Jesus feels so distant, so far away. It's not like how he felt before. And that is so lonely and so terrifying. But I can't give up. Maybe if I continue to talk, continue to plead, I can be freed from my torment. I know that Jesus died for the whole world, so maybe if I show him that I'm loyal and willing, he will forgive me for what I have become. If I try hard enough, maybe, just maybe I'll be able to return to his good graces. So I continue to talk.

CHAPTER FOURTEEN

Benji Finds the Answer

It was empty trail after empty trail. Trying to find answers and coming up with nothing. Asking my neighbors if they saw anyone who looked like me. All I got were a lot of strange looks and more confusion. I knew I needed to let April know that I probably wouldn't be able to make it to DePaul this semester. Finding the truth was the most important thing right now. I don't really know why it was, it just was.

I had never been this passionate about anything in my life. Not my dreams. Not God nor religion. To be honest, not even about April. It was like a war inside of me. I wanted to go to university, yet I needed to find the truth about myself. The truth about my existence and who I really was. And the only way I could do that is by finding my other half. It's funny but when I started searching for my twin, or whoever he was, I couldn't find him. I had seen him once, so I knew for sure that he existed. But it almost seemed like he knew I was searching for him and was now in hiding. That was the most infuriating thing of all. If we really were twins, didn't he want to know about me as well? Didn't he want to learn more about himself, as well? Where could he hide in such a small town? Or had he already left? I don't know but I continued to search.

I only had a few days left to find the answer. I just couldn't bring myself to tell April that I couldn't go to school with her right now. I knew that she would be understanding about my situation but for some reason, I just couldn't bring it up. It was like my mouth was continuously clamped shut whenever I was around her.

As my obsession grew, I started to have some terrifying dreams. In my dreams, I was with a woman, who was supposedly my mother, yet she always made me call her by her first name. She had adopted me, yet didn't even pay any attention to me. Every night, in my dreams, the story continued to unfold, laying out a horrible picture, where I was surrounded by drunken people who forced me to drink at a young age. Constant loneliness and isolation surrounded me, getting worse and worse every year. I even ran away from home, several times. Stealing, doing drugs, and drinking constantly. But I would always end up back in that terrible house. I also saw images of Jesus hanging on the cross, intermittently, throughout every dream. What was most shocking about that was even though his face was covered in blood, he was smiling.

But for some reason there was a shift in circumstances. In the very last dream I had, it seemed like I had finally become fed up with my circumstances, throwing a beer bottle at that woman's head. I knew in my dreamlike state that it was just a dream, but it honestly felt so real. The last thing I remembered in that dream, was a boy walking toward me with a bright smile on his face. He waved as he got closer. "Judah," he called. As he said that, I suddenly jolted awake. So it wasn't me. Was it my brother? Is this what he has been through? Was his life so devoid of love that he ended that awful woman's life? Where are you, Judah? Why can't I find you?

I knew, after that dream, that my time was up. I needed to tell April what was going on. I knew she would be disappointed but would understand my circumstances. After all, I've told her everything about myself. She would understand that I needed to find my brother, especially after everything I had seen in my dreams. My brother needed me.

I don't know how April would feel about him being a murderer, so I just wasn't going to mention that part. So with a trembling heart, I made my way over to April's house. As I made my way toward her home, walking this time, instead of riding my bike, I could see the faint outline of April walking with Adam, coming toward me. They both looked lost somehow, like small children who had just been scolded. Behind them was another boy, who I believe was the Donovans' nephew, James, or something like that. He also looked very downcast.

Their drawn faces scared me. Maybe they already found out I wasn't going to DePaul. I don't know. As I neared them, my heart was racing. I don't know why it was beating fast. It wasn't like I was committing some great sin or something. But something in me was filled with so much fear and honestly so much pain, that I had never truly felt before. The James kid, who was looking at the ground before, stopped to look into my direction. There was hurt in his eyes and he almost looked like he was about to cry. I had no idea why.

I barely knew him. I might have sat by him at church, before, but that's about it. Out of nowhere, in a loud voice, he called out to me. When he did, I instantly knew why he seemed so familiar. Where else I had seen him before. "Judah!" In that instant, I saw my last dream flash before my eyes, once again. James had been the one calling out to my brother. But this time he was calling out to me.

CHAPTER FIFTEEN

Benji and Judah

He said it once again. "Judah." I stopped in my tracks. April, Adam, and James continued to come closer, until they were right next to me. April looked like she had been crying. I could see anger in Adam's eyes, that I had never seen before. I looked at James as he intently looked back. Here might be the answer to all my questions. He knew Judah. Knew who he was and where he came from. He was the key that would unleash the truth. "Judah! Why aren't you answering me?!" James now was yelling at me.

I looked around me. I didn't see my doppelganger. I didn't see anyone else except for the four of us and a couple of birds sitting in the trees nearby. I finally spoke, my heart nearly about to explode in my chest. "Why do you keep calling me that? Who is Judah? Please. I need to know!" James stared at me, mouth agape. He looked utterly disgusted. "What kind of sick game is this? They already know who you are. You can stop pretending." He said motioning to April and Adam, who could barely look at me.

As I looked at the three of them, I realized this was all a misunderstanding. I was already confused by this entire situation, how much more so would they be. To have someone that looks exactly like you show up out of nowhere. That's confusing stuff.

If I tried to explain, I think everything could be worked out. Or at least, I hoped so. "I'm sorry but I think you have me confused with someone else." Before James tried to interrupt me, I continued. "I know this might sound crazy but I think you have me confused with my twin brother. My name is not Judah. It's Benji. I've grown up here my whole life. I met April and Adam, several months ago, but they already know that about me. They saw my parents and went to my house. That should be enough proof. I actually have been looking for Judah for the past several days." I directed my attention toward April. "That's why I've been looking for you. I can't go to DePaul this semester. I'm really sorry. It's just ... I need to find answers, about... well, Judah. I am guessing he is my twin, or brother, and we were separated. I never actually knew about him, until I saw him recently. When I was walking to your house for the barbecue, that was actually the first time I saw him. I'm sorry I didn't tell you about this sooner, it's just, I didn't want to hurt you. But I'm telling you now. I hope you can forgive me and understand."

April stared me at with her tear-stained face. Eyes filled with something I couldn't recognize. April let out a shaky breath, before closing her eyes. In the stillness she whispered, "Your name isn't Benji, is it." I looked at her, speechless. Had she not heard what I just said? She believed some guy, she had just met, over me? What is going on? I looked to my friend, Adam, for help but he wouldn't even look at me. "What's going on? Why don't you guys believe me? April, I thought we told each other everything? I know I withheld this information from you, but I thought it would confuse and upset you. I'm sorry I didn't let you know right away? Next time I'll be much more honest with you. Let's just go to DePaul, okay? We can figure everything out from there!"

April looked at me again, with confusion etched into her face. "I don't know where you got the idea that we were going to DePaul together. And to set the record straight, Adam and I never met your parents. You told us a lot about them, but we never met them, or even went to your house."

"April?" I couldn't believe it. Not only did she believe James, she also denied everything that we did together. All our memories. "What about us dating? You said you loved me. And I said I loved you too. Doesn't that mean something?"

April looked even more startled. "I've only known you for a month. We met for a free, one-week class at the local community college. You told me that you lived here your whole life... I should have realized that it was weird that I had never seen you before, in such a small town. You came to our church, got baptized, and met my parents. We have hung out before, but it wasn't serious. We were just starting to get to know each other. I did like you, but it was all just starting."

I stared at the three of them. With their faces filled with fear, anger, and sadness. I could feel a crushing weight in my skull, almost as if something was trying to get into my brain. No! I had to fight this doubt! I was Benji! No matter what they said, I was Benji! Something was seriously wrong! How could Adam and April look at me like that! Especially after everything we had been through!

In my mind I saw flashes of the dreams that I had been having. Dreams of Judah and his mother. The intense loneliness and pain. I saw the golden cross, once again, with Jesus hanging on it. Over and over again. Running and rushing through my mind. I saw Judah throwing the bottle at his mother, and I saw the dry blood that was there, caked on her face, the next morning. I saw James, once again, calling Judah's name. I tried so hard to push these images away. I'm Benji! I'm a good person. A person that God didn't have to forgive. A person that Jesus didn't have to die for! I was close to Jesus. And he loved me! I could never be Judah! I was good! I was kind to my family and friends and I loved April! I had never done anything seriously wrong and I had parents who loved me more than anything in this world. And would support me in everything! Judah was unfeeling, selfish, and a murderer. His own mother didn't love him. He was everything I was not.

James had to interrupt my thoughts. "Judah. I know this is hard for you to accept but it's the truth. You need to face your actions head on. You've been lying to so many people! And I understand why you did it. I know what you have been going through with your mom. And I know that you needed to get away."

He stopped for a second, letting out a shaky breathe. "I care about you, man, but we had to do what we did." I stared at him, even more confused. "I heard about your mom's murder. It happened on the night before you contacted me. I knew, when I found out, that I needed to let my uncle know. He said it was best to let the police know what had happened. So, yeah. They'll be coming soon. I'm sorry, Judah. But it had to be done." I felt my heart drop in my chest. Not only did they think Benji wasn't real, they thought I was an actual murderer. Me! I couldn't comprehend what was going on at all. Everything made no sense. How was this possible?

Everything seemed even more surreal, when the police came and I was handcuffed. I was not a killer! I did not deserve this type of treatment. I kept pleading with April and Adam to let the police know who I really was. That I would never do anything to hurt someone else! That I was Benji! But they didn't say anything. Didn't even look at me at all.

As I was taken away by the county sheriff, I continued to yell and plead with them to defend me. To do something! Anything! But they all just stood there. James was the only one looking at me. The other two just stared at the ground. James's eyes were filled with tears. Something in me felt like crying, seeing his face. I barely knew him but it hurt me inside. He was the one who had caused this whole mess but still it was painful to see him like that. Everything was painful.

I was forced into the sheriff's car, being told I had to stop yelling immediately. I turned to look out the back window as James, April, and Adam began to disappear. Nothing made sense. This whole situation was unbelievable.

From there began the most grueling twenty-four hours of my life. The questioning went on for what seemed like an eternity. The worst thing of all was the officers didn't believe me at all. That I was Benji. They wouldn't even let me get ahold of my parents. Telling me that I only had my mother and of course she was no longer living, since I had killed her. I tried to explain time and time again that I wasn't Judah. I was Benji. Judah was most likely my twin brother. I told them that I could prove it if only I could find him. The officers became more and more frustrated, as I became more and more frustrated. I wished this was all a terrible nightmare.

Where I could wake up back in my family's house, in my own bed. That April would still love me. And Adam was still my friend.

The officers had stopped the interrogation for a bit. I sat at the table, where they had previously interrogated me, head resting on my arms. One of the officers who had just left, had placed several photos of the crime scene on the table that I was sitting at now. I hadn't looked at the pictures earlier, because I hate gruesome things, and it wasn't my crime scene, so why should I have to look at it. After hours of interrogation and no rest, I decided just to look. Maybe, in some way it would help me to argue my case. If anything, it might help me get more information on who Judah really was.

I scooted my hand over, head still resting on my arm, flipping over the pictures. First picture was of a blood-stained chair. Second, shattered glass, from a beer bottle. And finally, the last picture. As I turned it around, I felt my heart drop, almost out of my chest. That woman's face. The one I had seen in my dreams. It looked so familiar and yet so different. Her face was so pale, lips almost white. Her eyes were shut tightly. Blood trailed down her face, neck, and onto her clothes. The blood had even gotten onto her precious armchair. The one she sat in every night and drank. As I stared deeper and deeper at the picture, I couldn't take my eyes off of her face. I remembered exactly how it had happened. How drunk I was and how much I hated her. I remember in my rage, throwing that bottle at her. This wasn't a dream anymore. This was reality.

Then the fear started to overpower me. What was I even saying? I wasn't Judah! I was Benji! Nice, innocent Benji! Who had loving parents and great friends! Everyone liked me! I was a good person! I wasn't this kind of person! I wasn't evil! I didn't hate anyone! I didn't have a mom who neglected me like this! This wasn't me.

Even though I fought it, wildly, the death of that woman, continued to flood my mind. As well, as many other images of Judah's life. I tried with everything in me to push them out. After that, the things I did not want to admit began to flood into my mind.

I never grew up in April's town. I had only come there a couple of month's ago, with James. April and I did meet in a free, one-week program at a community college nearby. Yes, I did go to her church, and I did get baptized, and yes, April and I did hang out together, talked about the future, our beliefs, hopes, and dreams.

I had to stop myself from thinking about all of this. It was too painful! But the truth continued to come forth. My parents, my wonderful parents, weren't really my parents. They were a couple I had met, during my nightly trips to James' uncle's church. Their house was near the church and they had invited me to have dinner with them. From there, I went fishing with my "dad" and went on walks with my "mom." They supported me with everything and even told me to call them mom and dad. I only knew them for a couple months but I wanted them to really be my parents and no one could tell me otherwise.

I began to realize that all this time I had told most of the town's people that my name was Benji. I said it, so it could eventually become reality. I also, eventually, started to believe the delusion. After saying it out loud, so many times. I wanted to hide everything that I truly was. Mask all of my sin and shame. Everything was going so well. I had almost got everything that I had ever wanted. Even creating my own extra fabrications, so that hopefully, they could one day become a reality. But of course everything had to come crashing down. Forcing me to face the ugly reality that I was in fact not Benji. To makes things worse, there was no twin. There was no brother, doppelganger, whatever. There wasn't even a Benji at all. There wasn't any goodness, purity, or innocence. Just selfishness, and evil. There was just Judah.

CHAPTER SIXTEEN

Just Judah

Everything went by so quickly after my realization. That there had been no Benji to begin with. After hours of interrogation, everything became clear. And it was evident that I couldn't escape the consequences of my actions, no matter how much I tried to avoid them and shift the blame onto someone else. I even made myself into another person. But no matter what I did I couldn't evade the past. I couldn't evade my guilt, my sin, and my overall unhappy life. I just couldn't. So I did what I needed to do from the beginning. I confessed what I had done.

I admitted my hatred for the woman who had raised me. I even confessed how my mother and her friends had treated me, as I grew up. Something I would have never admitted and said aloud, even just a few days before. But things had changed. What did I have to lose? I was probably on my way to prison, anyway. The confession was done. My guilt was confirmed. Now all there was left to do was wait for my trial.

I spent the night in a holding cell, in the small-town sheriff's station. I was the only one in the holding cell. It seems like this town doesn't have a lot of criminals. There was only one officer watching over me and he spent most of the night playing some game on his phone. Other than that it was silent. Very quiet.

I sat staring at the wall, at the other end of the holding cell. As my eyes traced the marks on the walls, probably from years of people coming in and out. Most likely bored out of their minds in this tiny cell. My eyes drifted upward until they reached the highest point of the wall. There hanging at that point was a golden cross, shining down on me. When I saw this, I instantly retracted my eyes.

I was too ashamed to look at it. I didn't have Benji anymore. I had nothing good left in me. How could I even look at that cross? After all that Jesus had done for the whole world. How could I face him? Benji was my only way of feeling even a little bit better about myself. Benji was the only thing that gave me a sliver of hope that I would be forgiven and that Jesus would once again smile down on me. How was I ever going to be in his good graces after this? I knew that I was going to end up in the fires of hell after all. With Benji I had a chance of maybe going to heaven, but those dreams were now dead.

But in the silence, I felt a stirring inside of me. Something that I had never felt before. Something I didn't understand but knew I had to listen to. It was urging me to ask for forgiveness once again. To confess once again. To look back at the cross. And so I did. But I didn't know what to say. I didn't know how to start. Or even how to form the words. So in the stillness, my heart beating intensely, I simply said his name. "Jesus."

As I gazed steadily at the cross, I heard something very clearly. Yes, I know what you're thinking. That I'm crazy. I don't blame you. I am kind of crazy. But it wasn't an audible voice. It wasn't even very loud. It was more like a feeling, or stirring deep inside of me. Right next to me. It was as close as my breath. So close, I could almost touch it.

That voice, as soft as a gentle breeze, stated, "I am here. I am right beside you." I felt my body begin to shake as I looked around me, seeing nothing. I spoke again. "How could you be right beside me? I've been talking and pleading with you for months and I heard nothing. No answer. I was so scared. So lonely. I tried to confess my sins but it was all in vain. No matter what I do I feel so guilty! I want you to love me but I know I'm no good! I know I don't deserve forgiveness, or love, or anything! I know that you'd rather have Benji than me! But he's gone now. I just don't know what to do! I give up! I surrender! I don't know what to do anymore! Help me!" I sobbed out. I didn't care if that officer heard me. I needed to hear the truth, no matter how much it hurt. I cried, in desperation, needing an answer.

In the same gentle stillness, I heard that stirring once again. "Judah. I love you. Not Benji. Just Judah." He loved me? He actually loved me? Why? Not even my own mother loved me. Nobody loved me. But God's Son, Jesus, did? How was that possible? I hated myself. How could he love a miserable, evil fool like me?

"Why?" I asked. "Why would you love me? Everyone hates me. Why would you love me after everything I have done. My own mom hated me up until the moment I killed her. Jesus, I killed her. I know you saw it already, but I did it. Why would you love me?"

"Because you are mine. I created you, I died for you. Through my death and resurrection, you no longer are parted from me. I will always be with you until the end of time. I am your God, your Father, your brother, and your friend. Nothing can separate you from me. Not even murder. You are mine and I am yours. Just come to me and accept me as your Savior. You will be free to leave the old Judah behind. Benji is no longer needed. He was never needed. I am all you need."

He said "I am all you need." He said I can leave the old Judah behind. I can leave behind my mistakes, my failures, my sins. I can leave behind the pain of my childhood. The pain of never being loved. The pain of who I was becoming. He said he was my Father and my friend. I had never had a Father, until now. I had never had a friend who said he loved me, until now.

Once again I spoke into the stillness. "I'm sorry. I'm sorry for everything. Forgive me! I want you to be my Savior, Father, and my friend forever. I believe in your death and resurrection. Please stay by my side forever. Thank you . . . For loving, for actually loving me. Thank you."

I felt something I had never felt before. It was like a flame burning in my chest. But it wasn't painful. It was warm and gentle and filled with life. I was on fire, yet safe. And filled with an overwhelming feeling. It consumed my mind and my whole body. Every part of me was covered by it. It was a mix of peace, and stillness, and excitement, and many other things I couldn't name, because I had never felt them before. In the midst of it all, I heard that gentle voice again. "Your sins are forgiven. You have been set free. I am here and will always be here. Right by your side. You are my son. My Judah. And I am your Father. I love you, my son."

The End.